WELCOME TO
PASSPORT TO READING
A beginning reader's ticket to a brand-new world!

Every book in this program is designed to build read-along and read-alone skills, level by level, through engaging and enriching stories. As the reader turns each page, he or she will become more confident with new vocabulary, sight words, and comprehension.

These PASSPORT TO READING levels will help you choose the perfect book for every reader.

READING TOGETHER
Read short words in simple sentence structures together to begin a reader's journey.

READING OUT LOUD
Encourage developing readers to sound out words in more complex stories with simple vocabulary.

READING INDEPENDENTLY
Newly independent readers gain confidence reading more complex sentences with higher word counts.

READY TO READ MORE
Readers prepare for chapter books with fewer illustrations and longer paragraphs.

This book features sight words from the educator-supported Dolch Sight Words List. This encourages the reader to recognize commonly used vocabulary words, increasing reading speed and fluency.

For more information, please visit www.passporttoreadingbooks.com

Enjoy the journey!

D1040538

Little, Brown and Company

Hachette Book Group
237 Park Avenue, New York, NY 10017
Visit our website at www.lb-kids.com

Little, Brown and Company is a division of Hachette Book Group, Inc.
The Little, Brown name and logo are trademarks of Hachette Book Group, Inc.

The publisher is not responsible for websites (or their content)
that are not owned by the publisher.

First Edition: September 2013

ISBN 978-0-316-22831-2

Library of Congress Control Number: 2013932903

10 9 8 7 6 5 4 3 2

CW

Printed in the United States of America

Passport to Reading titles are leveled by independent reviewers applying the standards developed by Irene Fountas and Gay Su Pinnell in *Matching Books to Readers: Using Leveled Books in Guided Reading*, Heinemann, 1999.

Meet Boulder the Construction-Bot

Adapted by **Annie Auerbach**

Based on the episode
"Walk on the Wild Side" written by
Nicole Dubuc

LITTLE, BROWN AND COMPANY
New York Boston

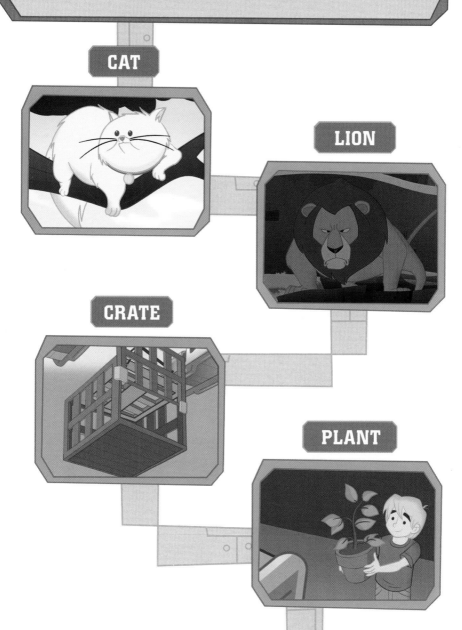

Attention, Rescue Bots fans!

Look for these items when you read this book.

Can you spot them all?

CAT

LION

CRATE

PLANT

The phone rings in the firehouse.

"Emergency!

Come right away!"

the chief hears the caller say.

"It could be a fire!" says Dani.

"Or a broken pipe!" says Graham.

The Rescue Bots change form.

The humans jump inside and go.

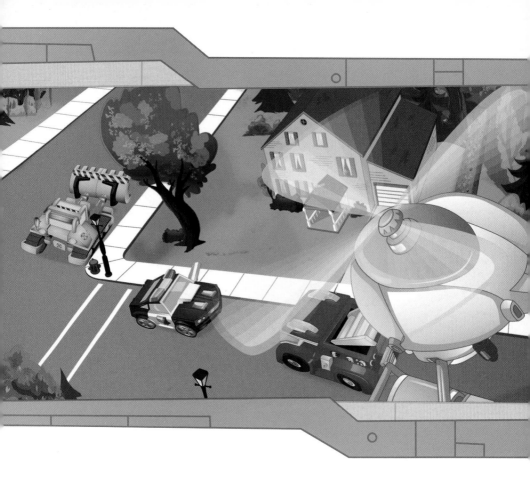

They arrive at a home.

What a surprise!

It is just a cat stuck in a tree!

Boulder changes back into a robot.

He helps the cat climb onto his body.

The owner is happy.

Later, Boulder asks Cody about pets.

Cody thinks pets are very cool.

"Some pets even work on rescue teams,"

Cody says.

"Wow!" says Boulder.

Now Boulder wants to get a pet

for the rescue team.

He wants it to be a surprise.

So Blades and Boulder sneak out at night.

Boulder wants to find a pet
at the zoo!

The gates are locked.

Boulder turns off the power.

The gates unlock

and all the cages open.

"Look!" says Boulder.

"Here is the perfect pet!"

He points to a large lion.

It reminds him of the cat
that he rescued.
"We can call it Whiskers,"
says Boulder.

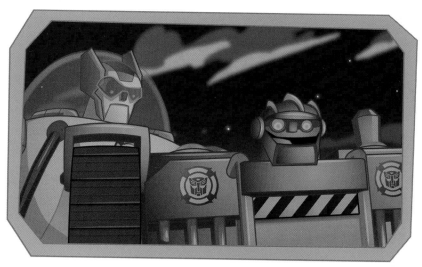

The lion roars.

It leaps out of its cage

and into a tree.

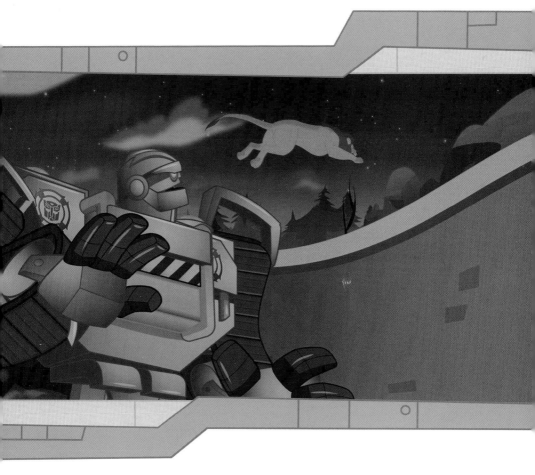

Then it jumps over the zoo wall.

The lion has escaped!

The next day,
Chief Burns gets a call for help.
He and the rescue team rush out
to find the lion in a tree!

"We found my pet!"

says Boulder.

"That is no pet,"

Graham says.

"That is a wild animal.

It needs to go back to the zoo!"

Boulder looks sad.

"Human ways are so confusing,"
says Boulder.

The lion jumps from the tree.

Chase tries to grab it but misses.

The animal runs down a busy street.

The team must catch the lion!

"Rescue Bots,
roll to the rescue!"
says Heatwave.

Boulder drives up on one side
of the lion.
Heatwave drives up on
the other side.

The lion snarls and growls.

It is trapped.

"Now!" shouts Graham.

Blades drops down a huge crate.

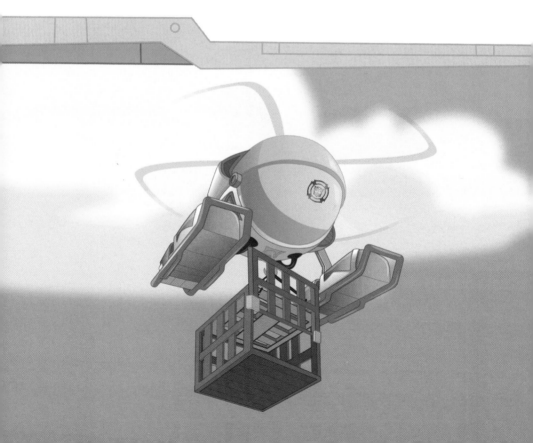

The lion is locked in the crate!

"Great catch!"

says Cody.

The animal is put back
in the zoo.
The mayor makes sure
the cage is locked.

"Whiskers was too much work,"
Boulder tells the team.
"But it would be nice
to have a pet."

"I know how you feel,"
says Cody.
"So I got you something
to care for."

Cody hands Boulder a plant.
"Come on, boy,"
Boulder says to the plant.
"Want to play catch?"

Cody laughs and shakes his head.

"Boulder!" he says.

"Plants do not play catch!"